EAST HADDAM P.T.O.

CLUCK. CLUCK

AT GRAMMY'S HOUSE

by Eve Rice

illustrated by

Nancy Winslow Parker

Greenwillow Books, New York

For Nate—who is
and wonderful—with all my love
—E.R.

For Great-Aunt Unia
—N.W.P.

The endpaper designs are adapted from two American pieced-quilt patterns:
left, "Streak o' Lightning," Pennsylvania, 1880; right, "Nine Patch Block," Pennsylvania, 1900.

Black pen, watercolor paints, and colored pencils were used for the full-color art. The text type is Clearface Regular.

Library of Congress Cataloging-in-Publication Data
Rice, Eve.   At Grammy's house / by Eve Rice; pictures by Nancy Winslow Parker.   p.   cm.   Summary: A brother and sister spend a delightful day at Grammy's farm.   ISBN 0-688-08874-0. ISBN 0-688-08875-9 (lib. bdg.)   [1. Grandmothers—Fiction.
2. Farm life—Fiction.]   I. Parker, Nancy Winslow, ill.   II. Title. PZ7.R3622At 1990   [E]—dc20   89-34617   CIP   AC

On Sunday afternoons,
David and I walk over the hill...

to Grammy's house.

Grammy grew up
on a farm, far away,
and she says,
"Bonjour, bonjour!
Comment allez-vous?"—
which is French for
"Hello! Hello!
How are you?"—
when she greets us
at the door.

Grammy has a stripey cat named Mimi and a dog called Pierre who sleeps under the stairs. Her house smells good, of old lace and baking cakes.

She hugs us both and says,
"I've saved the last bit of icing for you."

Grammy gives each of us
a wooden spoon covered
with warm chocolate icing.

We can hear
Grammy's cow
mooing by the
kitchen window.

We help Grammy milk the cow and bring back
a pail full of milk, topped with fresh cream.

At Grammy's house, we make butter the
way they did when she was a little girl.
Grammy hands me a big jar of cream.

I shake it and shake and shake…
until, suddenly, there is a lump of
yellow butter in the jar.
"That will be nice on our muffins for
supper," Grammy says, as David
spoons it into a dish.

CHUG!

We hear a tractor drive up and look
out the window to see Uncle Jack.

. 14 .

"Hello, everyone," he calls. He opens the screen door and goes straight to the sink to scrub the grease from his hands.

In the hallway, Grammy brushes my hair and braids it
into one long braid, right down the middle of my back.

"Now, let's wash up—quick!" Grammy says to David
and me, and then it is our turn at the sink.

. 18 .

We dry our hands and help Grammy set
the table. Her dishes have little flowers
on them and are very old.

Grammy takes the meat from the oven.

It sizzles in the pan while she mashes the potatoes.

Then she makes the gravy.
"Watch," she says, and
in a minute more,
"There—it's done!"

Then everything is ready.

We all sit down at Grammy's table. She puts meat and carrots and mashed potatoes on our plates. We say a blessing and pass the muffins and the butter—"Yummmmmm."

When the plates are cleared, Grammy brings out
the best chocolate cake in the whole world.
"Little slice or big?" Grammy says—even though
she knows we <u>always</u> ask for "BIG!"

KNOCK,
KNOCK

Then David and I help Grammy do the dishes in the
big kitchen sink. But before the last dish is dry,

there's a knock at the door. It's my mom and dad.
They've come to take us home.

"Good-bye, good-bye—and thank you,"
we say. David and I kiss Grammy
and Uncle Jack on both cheeks.

Grammy hands us some cake wrapped up in foil.
"Good-bye," she says, and "Au revoir!"—which is
French and means "Till I see you again."

"Au revoir! Au revoir!"
we call, as we go
down the walk,
"Till we see
you again…
next Sunday!"

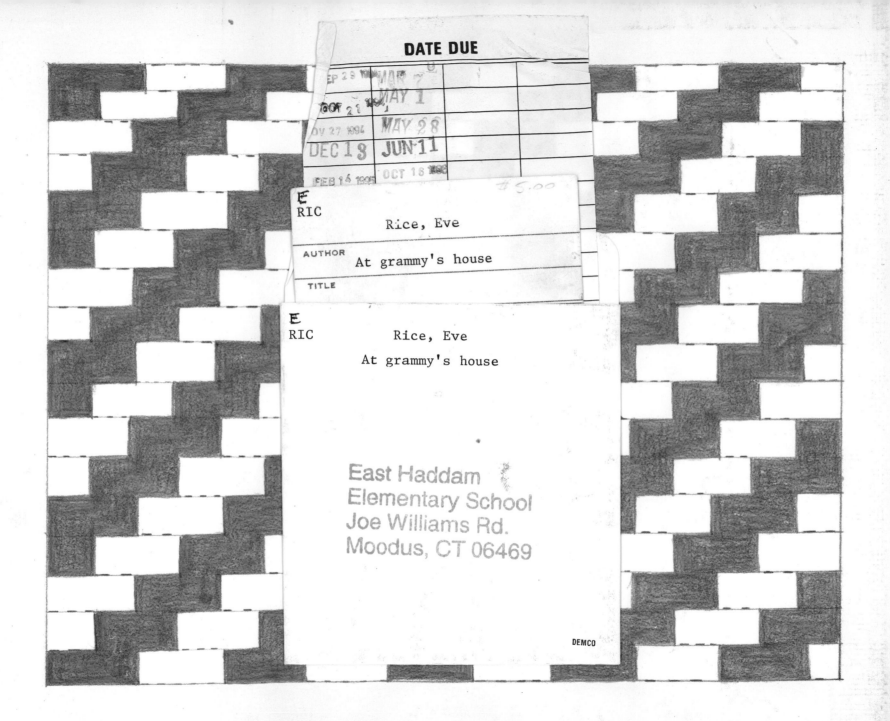

E
RIC   Rice, Eve

At grammy's house